IRON VIKINGS MC - PREQUEL

ANNA CASTOR

ANNA CASTOR

ISBN: 9789083172231

Developmental Editing by Lauren Griffin

Proofread by Roxana Coumans, Roth Notions Book Editing Service

INTRODUCTION

GLOSSARY:

Brother: Fully patched member of the Iron Vikings MC.

Church: Meetings for officers of the club, led by the President.

Cut: Leather vest worn by members. Patches stitched onto a member's cut indicate their club, chapter, position, and other achievements.

Enforcer: Works together with the Sergeant-at-Arms to keep the club safe. He is the club's muscle to dole out punishments.

Iron Viking: Member of the one-percenter motorcycle club Iron Vikings MC.

Old Lady: Girlfriends and women with wife status belonging to a club member.

One-percenter: Outlaw bikers who live by their own rules.

Out in bad standing: When a member is banished from the club for violating club rules.

President: Leader of an Iron Vikings Chapter. They vote all club decisions at the table during Church, but the President's word is binding.

Prospect: Like a pledge in a fraternity, prospects have to earn their cut and become a fully patched member. This period in which they have to show their loyalty and do anything that is asked of them by club members takes up to at least eighteen months.

Road Captain: Responsible for planning runs and rides at the front of the formation whenever the President or Vice-President is absent on the ride.

Road name: A moniker given to a club member by his brothers. Often as a reminder of an event or trait that was impactful, meaningful or straight up funny.

Run: A ride for club business. Sometimes the MC organizes a charity run or a run out of state for biker events.

Secretary: Makes and keeps all club records. Spreads the word about the decisions at the table to the other members of the MC. Notifies Officers of emergency meetings.

Sergeant-at-Arms: Works together with the Enforcer to keep the club safe. Responsible for keeping order and protection of the club.

Sweetbutt: A woman who voluntarily stays at the clubhouse or comes to parties to service the club members. Mostly sexually.

Treasurer: Responsible for keeping a record of the club's finances.

Vice President (VP): Second-in-command and the intermediary between the President and the members and prospects. Responsible for the maintenance of the clubhouse building and the bar management.

IRON VIKINGS MC

President: Annas
Vice President: Silas
Sergeant-at-Arms: Zeus
Enforcer: Demon
Secretary: Tiny
Treasurer: Turtle

Road Captain: Red

Full Patched Members: Angel, Arrow, Blade, Bondi, Buzz, Crusher, Devlin, Doc, Fox, Ghost, Hunter, Kid, Mud, Mammoth, Phoenix, Vic, Wolf and Zion.

Prospects: Squirrel, Jason, and Evan.

Old Ladies: Marie (Old Lady of Tiny), Jessica (Old Lady of Red) and Ammeline (Old Lady of Zeus).

Sweetbutts: Allison, Eve, Gisele, Molly and Zara.

1

At the sandy altar, Zeus cradled the lifeless body of his fiancée, Ammeline. Her wedding dress turning a deep shade of crimson as blood seeped into the white lace-fabric. Zeus' eyes combed through the crowd of frantic wedding guests. He spotted his two sisters as they ran for safety into the beach club.

He took a deep breath, the scent of sea spray, and Ammeline's perfume engulfing him under a treacherous calm blanket in the eye of the proverbial storm.

He had tried to hold up Ammeline's body after that first bullet hit her heart. The second and third bullet to her stomach had no use for her murderer other than to delight in their success at hitting her on the first attempt.

The entire MC drove almost six hours from Austin to this quaint Texan beach town, nestled at the Mexican Gulf, all to make Ammeline's dream come true.

In a sick way, he was thankful he at least had given her a taste of her picture-perfect wedding day. Right until someone fired three rounds at his Old Lady before they even had a chance to say 'I do'.

"Get your motherfuckin' hands off me," he roared at someone jerking his shoulders.

He grabbed a stronger hold of her wet waist, his fingers slippery from her warm blood. Several hands lifted him off the ground and he tried to dig the heels of his polished boots deeper into the sand.

"It's not safe, Z. We need to go, man."

He recognized the voice of his best man. Demon wasn't one to hide or run from trouble. That he'd intervened so they could do so said a lot about their critical situation.

Zeus snapped out of it. He hadn't seen a shooter. Someone must have targeted Ammeline from one of the rooftops of the small businesses adjacent this private beach. There was no other way.

With Ammeline in his arms, he got up from the sand and made his way to the beach club where he'd stood inside just five minutes ago with sweaty palms, before he'd walked outside, cheered on by his club.

Demon pushed the glass doors open, waiting for Zeus to pass. He stepped in, high-pitched cries and shouts from his club brothers and sisters instantly washing over him. Doc stepped forwards and held out his hands. "Let me take her for you."

"Not a chance in hell." He passed Doc and his father, Annas, peering out of the window of the ground floor foyer, gun in hand.

Zeus walked over to a corner of the open foyer for some space and wondered if he should open Ammeline's eyes to get one last look at her striking green eyes.

Fox came through the door. "They're gone."

Zeus heard him but kept his attention on Ammeline's face. He imagined her waking up like she used to in the mornings and grace him with one of her sweet smiles.

No matter what he'd been up to, how late he'd rolled into their bed; she would curl herself around him and smile.

Ammeline had been born into the Iron Vikings MC, just like him. She knew he wasn't always on the up and up. It was how things rolled in the club and she understood to never question him.

Her father Silas was the VP to Zeus' father Annas, the IVMC's President. Zeus' union with Ammeline had been set in stone, long before both had even been born. Both their Greek mothers had seen to that. With their mothers drawing their last breath over eighteen years ago, he hadn't dared to question their wishes.

He'd been damn lucky Ammeline grew up into a looker—and sweet as hell. Too damn sweet.

Fuck. Why did they target her? She wouldn't even hurt an ant crawling over her food.

He glanced up at the surfboard hanging from the wooden ceiling in the beach club, fighting back the burning tears.

He knew why they'd shot Ammeline out of the entire MC brothers and Old Ladies present at the wedding.

As the daughter of the VP, future daughter-in-law of the Prez and wife-to-be of the Sergeant-at-Arms, Ammeline never stood a chance. In her stunning white dress, she'd been an easy target for any skilled sniper.

Zeus forced himself to break away from taking in Ammeline's lifeless face. A few feet away Fox stood, waiting. Zeus nodded for him to speak.

"Wolf found rounds up on the roof of that restaurant." Fox said and pointed to the flat roof of Sal's Salsa and continued, "Damn sniper got three of us before Demon got to him."

Demon entered the beach club, gun in hand and blood smeared over his white dress shirt under his cut.

"He breathin'?" Zeus' father asked, stepping away from his guard at the window.

All heads turned to Demon. "Unconscious and tied up in the back of Squirrel's van."

Squirrel nodded and stepped outside, not waiting for the order to go back to his van and watch the sniper.

The prospect would make a fine brother in six months, Zeus

was sure of it. The women huddled at the far end of the beach club foyer, while the men waited on their President to tell them what to do next.

"Bondi, go after him. Don't want Squirrel alone with the one guy who can tell us who's responsible."

The Aussie nodded before his colossal frame left the crowded foyer.

His father trusted no one. Not before you'd proven your loyalty, over and over again.

Zeus took in a deep breath, filling his nostrils with the rusty, iron-like smell of Ammeline's blood.

He clearly wasn't ready to take over the gavel from his dad. Annas warned him not to go through with the wedding so close to cartel territory, but he'd been arrogant, thinking they could handle it.

Ammeline had never asked for anything. She put up with a lot of shit from him over the years. The club always came first. She understood.

So when she'd brought up this rustic beach for the wedding ceremony, he made it happen for her. And it led them into this death trap.

They lost three of their brothers.

Ammeline was gone.

It was all on him.

2

The pressure around Zeus' forehead tightened with every word spoken from his brothers in the sacred backroom of their clubhouse. He rubbed at the dull pain of yet another headache. For the past hour, they'd discussed if they should exact revenge. Again.

His fingernail scratched at the Viking emblem carved in the hard wooden table before him. Their meetings had been all talk and no action for the past six months since they'd laid Ammeline to rest.

On that day, the club also held a memorial for their Secretary and Road Captain - Tiny and Red and their prospect, Jason. The sniper killed them before Demon caught up with him on the roof.

Unfortunately, the sniper had taken all his secrets with him to his grave. No matter what Demon and Zeus did to him—and they did some pretty gruesome stuff, the man held his tongue. In the end, Demon had cut off the man's tongue and fed it to him just before he choked to death.

"We can't risk it, Prez. I say enough is enough," Turtle said.

The treasurer would never risk anything. His road name said it all. If he could, Turtle would retract his ugly head in his shell at every chance encounter with danger. His position as a club officer had come easy. He grew up in the same neighborhood as Annas and Silas, the two founders of the Iron Vikings MC in 1979.

Zeus couldn't find one leadership quality in the almost seventy-year-old, and it irritated Zeus more often how Turtle had no working brain cells left in his skull after smoking weed and drinking every day for decades on end.

There were other guys in the club, like Zeus, who were ready to step up and take over from what was left of the mess the older generation had made.

Unlike the assumptions from most of his brothers, the first thing on Zeus' agenda as President wouldn't be revenge on the cartel. Sure, if the opportunity would present itself, he would be more than happy to make ground meat of the men responsible for Ammeline's death.

But since the wedding massacre, he had woken the fuck up. He put his personal vendetta on the side because there were bigger fish to fry. Or rather, he needed to get rid of the fish that had gone bad and stank up the pond, taking up all the oxygen.

He'd been a lousy Sergeant-at-Arms in this past year. The death of his Old Lady, two club officers and a prospect, uncovered what'd been going on right under his nose.

When he lost Ammeline, Zeus submerged himself even more in the club. The brothers he was closest with were there for him, hanging out at the club at all hours of the day.

And they noticed little things that didn't add up. Like his father's confusing mood swings. He barely ate the home cooked food at the clubhouse, slowly wasting away into some kind of zombie. And if it were even possible, Annas' fuse had gotten even shorter, fizzling around the clubhouse with his VP, like they'd been partying for four days straight.

And then last night, Zeus saw Silas snorting coke behind the bar when almost everyone stood outside for a fight. It shocked

Zeus to see their VP blatantly disrespecting one of their club rules inside their own clubhouse.

Two members had died from a drug overdose a decade ago, and since then the club stuck to growing, dealing and using weed only. Anything else was out of line and could send a member out in bad standing.

The only old timer at this officer's table who hadn't changed a bit was Turtle. The fossil liked his weed too much to try out any harder stuff and go against club rules. Turtle may be a useless club officer, but at least Zeus knew what to expect from him.

"I know you want your revenge, Zeus. But you can't drag the rest of the club down along with you on your ego trip," Turtle said while rubbing his chest long gray beard.

The stupid ass thought he was still dead set on putting a few holes in some Mexican drug lord. If he weren't such a scared little bitch, Zeus would have thought Turtle was in on it.

Zeus noticed Silas and his father shared one of those looks he had come to see in a different light recently.

In the first few weeks after Ammeline's death, Zeus couldn't live with the guilt. It tore him apart that if it weren't for his wedding at that damn beach, four people would still be alive today.

Every day at the office of Vikings Auto Salvage, he ran into Red's widow, Jessica, who worked as his and Demon's assistant. She just started dating some pencil pusher outside of the club. Zeus guessed it wouldn't take long before she would hand in her letter of resignation, fully embracing civilian life in a white picket fenced house with a fuckin' labradoodle.

That shit would never be Zeus. Ammeline had known as much from the get-go. The foundation of their relationship had been laid on their mothers' last wishes. Over time, Ammeline and him had learned to make things work.

She'd accepted his need to run free and never nagged him about it. Just like he never did on the few occasions she had her own nights of fun with guys outside their biker world or with a particular sweetbutt.

Even though he'd never been *in* love with Ammeline, he had loved her for the sweet and caring person that she was. When she'd suggested tying the knot at some beach, he didn't want to be that ass that'd deprived her of the dream wedding. It was the least he could do for her. Deep down, he knew she'd gotten the short end of the stick with him.

Turtle's sneer about Zeus taking everyone down with him left room for Silas, Ammeline's father, to look down his nose as he said, "Nobody loved Ammeline as much as I did. But it ends here."

Silas knew exactly how Zeus' guilt about not giving Ammeline everything she'd deserved was his one sore spot. Silas enjoyed rubbing it in. Sick bastard reveled in Zeus' struggle with his fucked-up emotions about Ammeline.

It didn't matter how unconventional their relationship had been. Or that he never would have loved her like she'd deserved. If it weren't for the attack, he would have married his childhood friend, Ammeline, the girl he grew up with in this club. The girl that trusted him to protect her from all the evil in their world.

During one of his many late night binge drinking at the clubhouse, Turtle said something that caught the attention of Zeus. Under a drunken stupor of beer and pot, Turtle let it slip that Silas was the one who'd brought up the idea of that beach location as their perfect wedding venue. Ammeline told Zeus she'd found pictures of the place on the Internet, never once bringing up it was her father's idea.

Red, their Road Captain, had arranged several runs to the remote beach to check up on things before the wedding. In hindsight, Silas, Red, and Zeus' father must have been smuggling drugs for over four months before the attack.

Zeus tried to concentrate on the meeting unfolding in front

of him. He glanced over at Demon, sitting opposite of him at the table. Demon's jaw ticked. That was never a good sign.

Demon earned the role of enforcer eight years ago at twenty-four. His life always revolved around survival through fighting. First at home, against his drunken father. Later, out on the streets whenever he got kicked out of the house for a night or two, standing up for his little brothers and sisters.

Demon nodded approvingly at Zeus when he ignored Silas' jab. An understanding passed between them. They were sitting on this secret and needed to hold on for just a while longer. Just so they can smoke out any other traitors before taking over the reins.

Demon had found packages of drugs in a hidden compartment in Red's closet as he'd been helping out Red's Old Lady, Jessica, when she moved out of her and Red's room at the clubhouse two nights ago.

Demon hid the drugs and confided in Wolf and Zeus about what he'd found since there was no way that Red had gone rogue, getting involved in hard drugs all on his own. The man never took a dump without asking their Prez first.

After this find, Demon and Zeus turned to their fellow club brother, Fox, to do some research. Fox used his hacking skills against his own Prez but he had yet to come up with hard evidence of the VP and Prez' involvement in selling blow.

Zeus let out a derisive snort at the memory. Like he needed any hard evidence. Staring at him from across the table, his dad was a shadow of the man he used to be.

"Zeus, we're not going against the cartel. We haven't got the manpower to make it out alive. We're lucky as it is they haven't retaliated for offing their hired sniper. For the last time; forget about it." His father's voice held an eerie undertone.

Zeus still held love for his father.

Maybe that's why he drank so much lately. He tried to drown his love for the man who'd cared for him and took him on camping trips after his mother died when he was just a fourteen-year-old punk.

He did his best to forget about his love for his father, because the man he used to know didn't exist anymore. Annas had betrayed the club the moment he secretly ran drugs for the cartel. It had brought them nothing but death and deceit.

When he didn't immediately respond, his father, Annas, slammed his fist on the table. "Enough! I've been too soft since you're my son. Not anymore. If you don't clean up your act, you're out. And you can take your fuckin' BFFs with you."

Zeus knew that his father purposely spoke about his 'BFFs.' He wanted him to know he saw them coming from a mile away.

When he still didn't react, Annas had enough and stood from his chair, pointing a finger at his own chest. "I'm still the President of this club. What I say goes. If you don't like it—you get the hell out of my club."

Zeus had to fight the urge to have it all out with his old man.

Right here. Right now.

Maybe that's why Demon also stood from his seat and said, "Let's cool off this weekend at the bend. We'll come back on Monday and talk. That okay with you, Prez?"

Annas' grunt wasn't exactly an answer but Demon patted Zeus' shoulder and they exited church. They stopped by the bar to grab their cell phones from the box under the counter where Squirrel kept an eye on the phones and cleaned up shit at the bar while the officers were in church.

As they stepped out into the blistering Texas air, Zeus said. "Fuckin' brilliant plan. What in the hell are we goin' to do all weekend long at the bend?"

At just an hour's drive away, there was this perfect spot at the Colorado River, right at a small bend. The place held enough privacy for partying bikers to camp out at.

Demon shrugged. "Take some weed, a few sweetbutts, and our closest brothers with us. The men can use a party until we go back and face the music, brother. It's not goin' to be easy to get everyone on our side during a vote—or worse."

His best friend had a point. They had found the drugs. They had their suspicions about the involvement of their VP and Prez. It may not be enough to overthrow hierarchy, however.

They needed more of the younger generation at that table. In the light of things, Demon's idea sounded not so bad. "Okay, let's round up some people."

Zeus paddled his inflated ring floaty closer to his other best friend, Wolf, several feet away in a small bend of the Colorado River.

"You make one hell of a sight, brother," he said before angling his floaty next to Wolf's flashy pink unicorn floaty.

Zeus could count the amount of brothers that would trade their spot for Wolf's unicorn on zero fingers. Wolf didn't give a fuck what others thought of him. He splashed some water in retaliation, but Zeus didn't mind the cool reprieve.

Zeus looked over at the shore, littered with partying brothers and sweetbutts. There were all types of girls hanging around the club. A few of the girls initially came to the club with no place left to go, willingly staying at the clubhouse in exchange for their services.

The club had its usual cut chasers who would hang around for years, hoping to become an Old Lady, settling down with a member. But the ultimate sweetbutts who didn't give the men any headaches were the girls who just liked to get fucked hard and put up wet. The spirit animals of some of Zeus' brothers.

As he watched Fox horse around with some girls in the water, he acknowledged how hard they all needed this brief break from the troubles in the club.

This new generation was sick and tired of the originals making a mess out of things, not showcasing any true leadership after the attack. Wolf, Demon and Zeus took over Vikings Auto Salvage after Tiny and Red died in the attack; unbeknownst to the chaos they'd left of the office and administration.

And IVMC's strip club, the Pink Flower, had also seen better days. Some dancers failed drug tests in the past month and had to be let go. Several of the club's best dancers jumped the sinking ship, leaving the stage for the club's inexperienced and less popular dancers.

At least the officers had voted on Devlin stepping up and managing the Pink Flower. It was a hard pill to swallow for Silas to step back and leave Devlin in charge. With these recent changes in management of the IVMC businesses, Zeus wasn't sure what Silas and Annas were up to next.

"What's our next move, Z?"

Zeus opened his palm and let the cool water flow between his fingers. He put some extra thought into his answer. "I need you at my side when we take over, VP."

He shot a glance at Wolf. The guy had been there for him ever since they'd been six and Joey Patirelli thought he could take on Zeus at the schoolyard. Zeus didn't need Wolf's interference, but after he'd split Joey's upper lip, they quickly became best friends.

When Demon joined their school four years later, he'd wanted nothing to do with Wolf and Zeus. Or anybody else, for that matter.

Later that year, Zeus and Wolf walked home from school and spotted Demon in an alley, lying unconscious in a pool of his own blood.

His father had ingrained it in him to never call the cops, so instead, Zeus called his dad. Annas and two of his club brothers showed up since the neighborhood sat in their territory and a ten-year-old left for dead earned their full attention.

That morning, Demon had jumped through his bedroom

window from the second floor to escape his father coming at him with a knife before breakfast. The grass backyard broke his hard fall, and he'd dragged himself with a broken leg and a sprained wrist around the corner into the alley Wolf and Zeus took everyday on their walk to the school bus.

When Annas found out, Demon's father got his ass kicked into the hospital, never to be heard or seen of again. His mother took care of Demon's younger brother and sisters on her own with the help of the club.

Annas moved Demon into the spare room at Zeus' house and they have been brothers ever since. It felt good to have another guy in the house growing up with two younger sisters.

Still, his choice for Wolf instead of Demon as his VP came naturally. He trusted Wolf with his life and that he could lead the club if something ever happened to him.

Demon's monsters from his past still haunted him. He'd once let it slip that the only way to cope was to hurt those who had hurt others.

Wolf simply nodded when Zeus called him VP. No surprise there, but Zeus saw the appreciation in his eyes.

"Your old man will not take this lying down, Z. You'd better be damn sure about all of this."

Zeus knew he was ready to take over the gavel from his father, even through anarchy. This club, the older brothers… they helped raise Zeus and the others into the men they had become. Splitting up the MC between the old generation and Zeus and his guys would be irreversible.

It meant war.

He only hoped they could make his father see how low he'd sunken. How rehab for both Silas and Annas was the only solution for turning the tide.

In all fairness, he didn't expect them to accept their help. What addict would give up an almost unlimited supply of their favorite drugs while making the big bucks?

Maybe it was that fourteen-year-old in him that hoped against his better judgment that Annas would try to focus on getting better. Over the past year, his caring father, the strong but fair leader of IVMC, had become this twitchy, paranoia shell of himself.

Annas hadn't held onto his position as the President for decades by being a snooze. He knew something brew within the lower ranks. The drugs made Annas even more dangerous. He became a wild card Zeus couldn't read. Zeus hated how he thought of his father as a threat. But he had no choice.

This needed to be done.

If it weren't for his father and Silas, Ammeline would still be alive. The Prez and VP had lied to their brothers, who weren't in on running drugs for the cartel, putting all their lives in danger. How ironic that Annas Doukas passed on to his children and club brothers that trust and loyalty were all that mattered.

"I am ready. Are you?" Zeus finally said.

Wolf's trademark grin that had earned him his road name was his answer.

Zeus watched the newest sweetbutt, Allison, wearing nothing, wading through the water in a direct line towards Wolf's stupid unicorn. Her light blonde hair stuck out in the sun, almost demanding his attention away from her natural breasts, moving with every stroke in the clear water.

Wolf held out his hand and hoisted Allison aboard. She straddled his lap and wasted no second in rubbing her pussy against Wolfs' trunks.

"Hi, Wolf. Zeus…" Allison's gaze dropped from Zeus' abs to his erection straining against his wet trunks.

Zeus and Wolf had a reputation for double-teaming club whores before he officially got together with Ammeline. Because of his open relationship with Ammeline, he still had his dick sucked multiple times over the years.

Ammeline had a thing for sweetbutt Gisele and often invited

her into their bed. He often wondered whose head Ammeline rather had between her thighs. As long as she didn't fuck one of his brothers, he was cool with it. He sighed and looked up at the sky. It was times like this that he wanted to go back in time.

Had their relationship been a matter of passing time, that neither of them would have chosen if it weren't for their mothers? They probably hadn't envisioned this for their children when they had forged their match.

Zeus' two sisters gave him a lot of shit about his open relationship, declaring them both a fool for sticking around.

A groan from Wolf brought him back to the present. He watched Allison's blonde head bob up and down on his best friend's dick. Allison made him rock hard by slurping Wolf's cock down to the back of her throat.

Ride free - live free.

Another club motto he was thankful for. His brothers had never judged him for whatever or whomever Ammeline and Zeus did in their bedroom, or outside, for that matter.

Zeus' eyes roamed the shore and found Demon sitting by himself on a log, a joint hanging from his lips. He lifted his chin when their eyes met.

"Fuck, Z. This girl can suck some cock," Wolf groaned and Zeus recognized his friend's tell for almost being there. That, and the sound of this wet, sloppy blowjob next to him, made Zeus believe Wolf in Allison giving some good head.

Six months.

Ammeline had been the last woman to touch him. It hadn't felt right in some screwed up way. It wasn't like the sweet and open-minded Ammeline would have minded. But every time a sweetbutt tried something, he got a weird sick feeling to his stomach.

The groans coming from Wolf as he came made him almost say 'fuck it' just for Allison to relieve him from his built-up stress.

He wouldn't, however, give himself to just any woman after a half-year of abstinence.

Fuck no.

Zeus had no idea for what or rather whom he'd been waiting for, but his gut told him not to give in to his urges.

He dove into the water to cool off and emerged at the sound of his best friend laughing at him. He held up his middle finger before he swam to shore, not bothering to retrieve his floaty.

4

Demon threw another log into the bonfire before plunking down next to Zeus. At this time at night, the rest of his brothers were either fuckin' their brains out or sawing logs by the sounds coming from the different tents and sleeping bags scattered around.

"That new sweetbutt keeps givin' you the eyes, Z."

The crackling fire spat red-hot sparks into the night sky. Zeus stared at the dancing flames, the bright yellow heart of the fire turning orange at the tips.

"Not interested," Zeus said.

Demon stretched his legs in front of him and took a pull of his beer. After finally having a sweet moment of silence at their campsite, giggles emerged from the tent closest to them.

"Since when is blonde and busty not your type?"

The man was pushing him and Zeus knew better than to take the bait.

"You done?"

Demon chuckled. "Yeah. I'm done."

"I'm not seeing you jumping her bones any time soon. And don't tell me she hasn't tried to get with you."

With a shrug, Demon said, "She's not my type."

Zeus knew exactly who his type was.

"I know. She's not five foot three, doesn't have long, dark hair dipped in pink, and she definitely doesn't swear like a sailor unlike someone else we know...."

That seemed to sober Demon right up.

"You know better than to go there, brother," Demon said while rolling another joint.

Zeus often liked to tease Demon and made him feel uncomfortable about Devlin's younger sister Catriona's infatuation with Demon ever since she'd turned eighteen and tried to kiss him. Zeus had kept his mouth shut to the rest of the club and especially Devlin, about walking in on that disaster.

The eleven-year age gap stood in between Demon reciprocating Catriona's flirtations. That, and his loyalty toward her brother. However, Zeus had a feeling that the moment Catriona would turn twenty-one in a few months, Demon would finally go for her.

As the club's enforcer, Demon knew the club rules like no other. Nobody messed around with club wives, sisters, or daughters. But Zeus saw how Catriona's perseverance made it more and more difficult for Demon to keep his distance from her.

"You finally asked Wolf as your VP?"

Zeus nodded. He knew better than to push Demon. If he didn't want to talk about Catriona, he wouldn't. No matter how drunk or stoned he got. Zeus respected that.

"Before or after the blonde sucked his dick?"

Zeus laughed. "Before."

Demon and Zeus looked over their shoulder at Fox and Wolf loudly praising Allison for taking Fox up her ass while fucking Wolf.

"Nothing like a weekend at the bend, man," Zeus said, and chuckled.

Demon stuck a stick into the bonfire, rearranging some fallen logs. "Yeah. I can't help but wonder though..."

"What?"

"What are we goin' to do if Dragon isn't in?" Demon said.

Zeus swallowed the rest of his beer. "He's not answering his phone."

"Stupid asshole."

He had to agree with Demon.

Demon's cousin joined the club three years ago. Dragon did a tour in Afghanistan before he finally listened to Demon and prospected. He was in his second year as a full-patched member and if it were up to Zeus, Dragon would replace him as the Sergeant-at-Arms. Dragon had the fighting skills, the gun knowhow, but above all, he had the balls to set other brothers straight.

There was one problem, though. When Dragon didn't sign up for another tour, there weren't enough spots at IVMC Austin, so he prospected at IVMC Seattle where Zeus' cousin had just started another IVMC chapter. Dragon and his two Army buddies joined IVMC Seattle together.

Bringing in Demon's cousin to stand by their side during the coupe meant they also had to bring in the two extra brothers. They were both excellent brothers from what he'd heard, but bringing all three of them to IVMC Austin wouldn't go unnoticed.

"He's only transferring to Austin if Ace and Ranger also have a spot here. I had my reservations about that, but I agreed," Zeus said.

"I'd like to think we're not that pathetic to demand such things from a future Prez," Wolf said before sitting down on a log next to Demon.

"What initially worried me was that I don't need another three men favoring each other. We already have Zion and Crusher—" Zeus said before Demon interrupted him with a snort.

Demon clearly didn't want to hear what Zeus had to say

about their two club brothers, who not only liked to tag team the sweetbutts but also were into each other.

"My cousin isn't into that. And if he was, no fuckin' problem. They've fought side by side in some forgotten spot in the outskirts of the world. That means more to them than being club brothers."

Zeus took the bridge of his nose in between his index finger and thumb. "Exactly. We can't have brothers favoring brothers. We're one club. And when it comes down to a fight—and we all know we're heading for war—it shouldn't make a difference if you're standing next to Crusher, Dragon, you or me. We all have each other's backs. No favorites."

Wolf snatched the joint from between Demon's lips and said to Zeus, "Damn. You sound more and more like your father. Spoken like a true Prez."

Demon snatched his joint back from Wolf. "You're an inconsiderate ass sometimes, you know that?"

"It's all right," Zeus said. "He's right. I do sound like him. I only hope I don't follow his footsteps and do everyone dirty."

Demon scoffed. "Shut the fuck up. Like that's even in you. You may have trouble keepin' your dick in check just like your old man, and you may even look and sound just like him... But you'll never betray your brothers to snort ice and live it up like in that Al Pacino movie."

Zeus wondered if with the right woman—someone he was in love with and he'd picked to spend the rest of his life with, if he would still want an open relationship. This half-year without Ammeline had given him time to think. Maybe if his world wasn't about to turn upside down in the coming months, he would be ready to meet the true love of his life. Someone he would walk through fire for. The one he would cherish and keep all to himself.

Damn it. Regret was a toxic emotion. He hated to think about his childhood friend Ammeline in terms of regret. She deserved nothing but honor and respect.

"You talk too much," Demon said to Wolf.

"At least I talk. Dunno why we didn't give you Grouch or Growl as a road name...."

Zeus grinned, watching the two of them bicker.

"I'm goin' to head in and leave you two lovebirds to kiss and make-up," Zeus said and chuckled at his friends cussing him out as he sauntered off. He entered his tent, immediately noticing the white blonde hair sticking out of his sleeping bag.

"Get out."

Allison didn't even stir at his icy tone. He had enough of this new chick already.

He nudged her upper leg with his hand, and the only reaction he got was a manly snore.

He sighed. After grabbing his duffle bag from beside his air mattress, he joined his bickering friends at the bonfire again. Zeus wouldn't sleep in the same tent as Allison. If she attempted to wake him up with one of those sloppy blowjobs, he didn't know if he'd have the strength to pull her off.

He settled in on the hard ground, his bag under his head. Zeus placed his hands on his abdomen and stared up at the night sky.

What would his mom have to say about everything going down in her family? Was she disappointed in her son for conspiring against his father?

Or would she support Zeus, knowing that Annas was out of control and no longer the same man he was during their marriage?

His phone buzzed against his leg. After swiping the screen, he finally received the words he was hoping for.

Dragon: *We're on our way.*

Demon's slap to his back was the wake-up call Zeus needed. He'd slept horribly on the unforgiving dirt ground. And just when he'd dozed off, Dragon, Ace and Ranger arrived at ten in the morning.

"Who do we have to finger fuck around here to get a cup of coffee?" Dragon said after revving his engine. He laughed despite himself.

Demon and Dragon could pass for twin brothers, if it weren't for Dragon's hair being sandy brown and Demon's pitch black. But Dragon's cocky wisecracks were a dead giveaway: the resemblance between the two cousins stopped at their exteriors.

"What's up, Z?"

Zeus clasped Ranger's hand and slapped his back. "Good, brother. Glad to have you three with us."

The solemn brother out of the three nodded in thanks. "Dragon never shuts the hell up about this place, figured it was time to see what all the fuss was about."

"Your Prez up in Seattle think you three are on a break or something?" Wolf said after greeting Ranger.

Ace smirked. "Yeah. Something like that."

When Zeus pulled a brow, Ace added, "We told him I met this chick online, and I was dying to meet her."

"Which is the truth," Dragon added.

"Needed your friends tagging along to cheer you on?" Wolf chuckled when Ace's head sharply turned to him.

"Wolf? That your name?"

Wolf squared off at Ace, ready to pull out his dick and show him who got the biggest schlung around Austin.

Demon placed his hand on Ace's shoulder. "You've earned our respect for your service and for becoming a full patched member, but as the new guys, you start at the bottom of our totem pole, Ace. Think you can handle that when ya'll transfer to Austin?"

Zeus knew Demon's words were a hard pill to swallow for Ace when he took a moment before agreeing.

"Okay, since that's out of our way, let's get this Sunday started already," Dragon yelled, earning him cheers from several men and sweetbutts.

Zara, Allison, and Molly strutted over to the three Seattle brothers.

Zeus headed to the river, giving Dragon time to let off some steam before talking shop. Zeus emerged from his dive in the river, a breath of fresh air filled his lungs. He would never take this magnificent, secluded part of the river for granted. The stream of the river drowned out the loud voices of his brothers back at their campsite.

A dainty hand slithered upwards on his bare back. He whirled around with a scowl on his face.

Gisele giggled. "It's just me."

"What do you want?"

She brought her hand through her caramel-colored hair and shrugged. When the silence turned awkward, she said, "I figured we could have some fun?"

Seeing Gisele in the morning light, against the beautiful trees and in the serene water while Ammeline lay dead in the dark dirt, hurt his chest.

"Not happening, Gisele."

He wondered if she missed Ammeline at all. She'd loved eating out Ammeline's pussy. Her enthusiasm at sucking his Old Lady's clit was a turn on for the both of them. But had Gisele reciprocated Ammeline's feelings even a little?

The way Gisele kept trying to get him to fuck her brains out made him believe her feelings hadn't run as deep as Ammeline's. It had only taken a week after Ammeline's death for Gisele to knock on Zeus' door. He'd turned her down flat. No way he would go there with her now. No fucking way.

Gisele walked deeper into the river, hiding her naked cheeks from him. Somehow, it made her more attractive.

He was done with the sweetbutts and his brothers walking around naked and fucking out in the open.

When his father took him to his first IVMC party, he hadn't known where to look. He was fourteen and his mom had just died three weeks before.

Ophelia Doukas would have never wanted for her fourteen-year-old son to lose his virginity at his first club party with some club whore two times his age.

It was sick. He knew that now.

But back in those 'good old days', nobody seemed to pull a brow. In his dad's eyes, it even turned him into a man. It made Zeus feel dirty.

Gisele watched him over her shoulder, checking if her little show got to him.

"If you're not taking her up on her offer, mind if I do?" Ranger said while walking up to them. Gisele turned, showing them her perky little tits. He had to give it to the girl: she was a looker. He didn't even like her all that much. He knew she had a mean streak underneath all that beauty.

"She's all yours, man."

For a brief moment, Gisele's face fell before she put on an insincere smile for Ranger.

He walked away from them, joining Devlin, who sat on the rocks staring out over the water.

"You all right?" he asked Devlin.

Devlin sliced a pebble through the water's surface. It made three jumps before twirling down to the bottom of the river. "Nothin' I can't handle, Z."

Zeus knew this beast of a man; this underground MMA fighter would sooner tear off his own hand before holding it out asking for help.

"I know. But we're here for you anyway, Dev."

Devlin picked up another pebble, thumbing it before throwing it into the river.

Zeus had done this thousand of times with his dad on their camping trips. He picked up a small teal pebble. Instead of skidding over the surface, the pebble immediately sunk to the bottom, irritating Zeus.

"I guess you heard?"

Zeus nodded. Devlin's fellow MMA fighter for the MC's underground fight club, Ronan Mills, had been stabbed. Since he wasn't a member but just a friend of the club, Annas had only sent Turtle, Angel, and Wolf to visit him at the hospital. Not that it had stopped Devlin from checking up on his friend.

"Yeah. How's he holding up?"

Devlin threw another pebble, this one skidding even further over the surface.

"He's going to make a full recovery. Don't know if he's going to fight for us anymore, though. He's dating one of my half-sisters now. He's ready to settle down."

Zeus knew Devlin's brothers and sisters, but had yet to meet Devlin's five half-sisters, as Devlin still had to get to know them himself. He'd found out about his dad having an entire secret family on the side not that long ago.

"When are you meeting your half-sisters? Wasn't that planned soon?"

Devlin sighed. "We're meeting them next weekend at some farm in Austin."

"No shit?"

"Yeah, my cousin Jessie arranged it with my half-sister, Bree."

"So that arrogant Irish bastard might end up as your brother-in-law some day?"

They both laughed since the club respected Ronan for the champion fighter he is, but also liked to joke about Ronan's cocky attitude. Zeus knew his dad once held high hopes for Ronan prospecting years ago, but Ronan's oldest brother, Brennan, put a stop to that.

"So it seems. Maybe I can talk some sense into my half-sister." Devlin chuckled.

Dragon walked up to their spot at the river.

"Should I leave you to talk?"

Zeus shook his head. "Nah. Stay."

Devlin might not be an officer in the club, but Zeus respected and, above all, trusted the guy. He could talk with Dragon in front of him.

Devlin had proved his loyalty to the club over and over again. He was just another example of the club withholding the next generation's opportunity to take over.

"What about your four other half-sisters?" Zeus asked Devlin, picking up their conversation.

Dragon sat down next to them and asked, "You got sisters?"

He'd asked it innocently enough, but Devlin's eyes narrowed instantly, already acting like a protective big brother.

"The oldest Ryan sister, Caitlin, is an ex-cop, and moved to Colorado. The middle sister, Fianna, works with horses and Bree is a schoolteacher. Two sisters served in Afghanistan. One of them, Kera, now works in the ER in Austin, the other, Gwenn, works for Donovan Mills, the PI."

"No fuckin' way."

Devlin jerked his chin at Dragon. "What?"

Dragon stood, looking down at them before glancing back at the campsite.

"I need to tell Ranger and Ace."

"Tell them what?" Zeus also stood, glancing from Dragon to Devlin.

"I can't believe it. What are the odds that we served with your half-sister, Kera?"

Devlin stood from his rock. "Come again?"

Dragon smiled. "It's true. Didn't you say 'Kera Ryan', and that she served in Afghanistan? Kera worked as a medic during our tour. We never served with her sister Gwenn, though."

Dragon laughed before he said, "If you already want to punch me in the face for knowing your sister, then you'd better not talk with Ranger. Him and Kera—"

"Can we stop talkin' about my sisters? I don't want them involved in the club."

Zeus held up a hand. "I get it. You know I got two sisters of my own. Nobody touches sisters or daughters."

Dragon scoffed. "Too late for that, brother. It happened before we even joined IVMC."

Devlin growled his next words. "Well, now you know they're my sisters. So back the fuck off. From all seven of them."

Dragon took a step backwards with both hands in the air. "It can go both ways between Ranger and Kera. Either they'll jump each other's bones or rip each other's heads off. I would not get into the middle of that shit storm if I were you."

Zeus blew out a deep breath.

These three new brothers from Seattle already gave him a headache.

"Kera will forever be a part of our crew. I can't disclose what happened. All you need to know is that she saved our ass. Doesn't matter we've lost touch over the years. We'll never back the fuck away from our girl."

Zeus got in between Dragon and Devlin, holding them apart by placing his palms upon their heaving chests.

"All right. Both stand down, for fuck's sake. Dev, there's history there, but Dragon obviously respects your sister."

Dragon nodded. "Can't deny I didn't try to get with her when I first met Kera."

"What happened?" Devlin asked, narrowing his eyes.

Dragon chuckled and said, "She cussed me out. Set me straight from the get-go. I love her like a sister, man. And let me tell you this: if she had a dick, I would have taken her with me to join IVMC Seattle."

Devlin snorted. "Yeah, right."

Dragon took a step backwards and Zeus' hand fell.

"You don't believe me. But you'll see... She's the best medic out there."

All this talk about this woman picked Zeus' interest. Maybe the club could use someone assisting Doc.

It sounded like Kera Ryan could hold her own amid foul-mouthed, rugged men. And she even had their backs during a battle of some kind.

Between starting a war with his father and his guilt toward Ammeline, thoughts about adding some random woman to the club as a medic they could call upon needed to be set aside.

They walked side-by-side back to the campsite, when Devlin muttered, "Can't believe I've got five more sisters to look out for now."

"Man, you're fucked." Zeus swallowed back his chuckle.

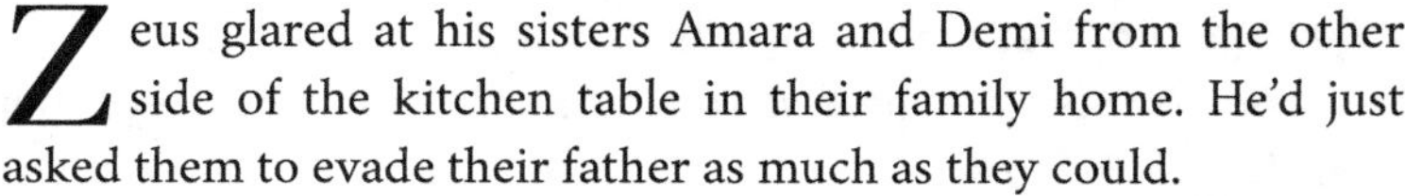

6

Zeus glared at his sisters Amara and Demi from the other side of the kitchen table in their family home. He'd just asked them to evade their father as much as they could.

He should have known better than to think they would listen.

"I don't get what's the big deal, Z. Dad's just going through a phase. Sure, he's partying more. Okay, he's embarrassing… But not more so than usual," Amara said, shrugging her shoulders.

He couldn't discuss club business with his sisters. It was up to him to keep them safe without giving them any details.

"Can't you two just do what I ask of you for once in your lives?"

Amara stood from the kitchen table and plunked her plate on the kitchen counter. She whirled around to give him a piece of her mind, her long, raven hair flowing before her green eyes for a moment.

She wiped the strands away and said, "What did you expect us to do when Dad crashed at the house? You know he lives here too, right? If he's not in his room at the clubhouse, he's here. And it's not like I have somewhere to crash. I don't have a room at your filthy clubhouse. And you and your buddies were away all weekend, screwing those sluts."

He didn't like to see his sister in pain. What she didn't say, but what he'd read between the lines, was that she obviously hated the idea of Wolf staying at the bend this weekend.

Zeus sighed. He should stay out of it. Wolf had no fucking clue Amara had a thing for him. Zeus only did because he knew his sister like the back of his hand. Wolf and Amara weren't dating. He was free to do whatever the fuck he wanted.

Hot anger flashed in Amara's eyes, like she knew what he was thinking.

"You guys disgust me. And here you are badmouthing Dad. You know birds of a feather flock together."

He stood from his seat and walked over to his sister. "Amara…"

His other sister, Demi, held his bicep and nodded to the kitchen window. "Z."

Somehow, he'd missed his father's hog driving up to the house. Zeus watched his father's legs eat up the long dirt path up to the wrap-around-porch.

"Shit."

The front door flew open with a bang, clinging to just one hinge to hold it up.

"Dad! Are you crazy!?" Demi shouted.

"Shut the fuck up, girl. I'm tired of you three tellin' me what to do. I'm a grown man. If I want to kick in the door to my own home, I fuckin' will."

Zeus took a step forward, strategically putting his sisters behind his back.

"You think you could stop me if I'd wanted to take a swing at the bitch?"

He cringed at his father's words. He never expected to ever feel this way, but Zeus was glad his mom wasn't alive. Cancer ate her up from the inside, but at least she didn't have to witness the love of her life stoop so low as to threaten her children.

"I don't know what the hell you're on, Prez, but you better think about this for a moment."

Annas' jaw tensed at Zeus calling him Prez instead of Dad. Or perhaps at being called out on his drug use.

"You want to be Prez so bad you can taste it, right?" Annas sneered. "I know all about your schemes, son. Callin' in three guys from Seattle. I can't believe I've raised such a back stabbing bitch. You disgust me."

Amara put her hand on his bicep. "W-what is he talking about? Zeus?"

Zeus didn't take his eyes off his father, and said, "Nothing, Amara."

Annas wiped a finger under his nostrils, laughing without humor.

"Ah, callin' in back up from IVMC Seattle is 'nothing'? We both know there's no fuckin' emergency to justify any of that. But your plan to get me out isn't goin' to work. You haven't got the votes."

Zeus already knew this. Demon's, and his vote stood against the three of Turtle, Silas and Annas. That's the whole reason Annas held off appointing new officers.

"We've been without Secretary and Road Captain for six months now. Why is that, Prez?"

Annas' eyes popped out of their sockets, shifted over his daughters before he focused on Zeus again. "I ain't discussin' club business in front of my daughters."

Good. At least he referred to them as his daughters this time.

"Let's go to the clubhouse, discuss it there." Zeus wanted to get him out of the house. Pain seared through his heart, realizing he didn't trust this drugged up version of Annas Doukas around his sisters.

His dad waved Zeus' idea away. "I ain't goin' nowhere. Who paid for this house, anyway? I'm crashin' here. I'm beat. Tomorrow, Silas and I are leaving for a couple of days."

"What for?"

Annas waved his question away, "Nothin' for you to worry your pretty head about."

Zeus couldn't believe this flighty, unbalanced man was his father. "Dad… Maybe we should—"

"Go back to the clubhouse, Z. You want me out? You go out there and round up your fan boys. I'm not taking this shit lying down. I'm the motherfuckin' President. Built this club from the ground up. And now my wet-behind-the-ears son wants to push me out?"

Zeus scoffed at his father, disregarding him being over thirty and far from wet-behind-the-ears.

Annas turned around and walked into the hallway, shouting, "Don't come cryin' when it backfires and you're booted out of my club. And y'all better leave me the fuck alone while I take a nap."

"He's high as a kite," Demi said to herself while they heard Annas stumble upstairs.

Zeus placed his arm over her shoulder, but she instantly shrugged him off.

"It's all because of that stupid club! If it weren't for IVMC, Dad wouldn't walk around like a junkie on a Monday morning!"

Demi had left home four years ago, following her boyfriend when he got a job as a cook on a cruise ship in Florida. She'd never understood the appeal of club life. She had always been more like their mother: soft and sweet. But not anymore. He'd noticed the change in her after her move to Florida.

He loved her, but he was glad Demi was only visiting. Demi had her own life in Miami and he didn't have to worry about getting her out of dodge in the coming months. It was his youngest sister, Amara, whom he couldn't beat away with a stick from the club that worried him.

She and Annas had always been two peas in a pod. If Amara were a guy, he was sure his father would have favored Amara above him to take over the club one day.

Zeus sighed and brought a hand through his thick black hair.

Before he could start, Amara beat him to it and said, "This is not about the club, Demi. This is about Dad being a total dick. Zeus and Demon are part of the club you hate so much. You know they're good guys. And you're not seeing them snortin' the snow from the driveway."

Demi scoffed. "That's one way of putting it."

"I don't have to remind you that what's been said should—"

Amara rolled her eyes and slapped the back of his head. "Geez. Give us some credit, Zeus."

He pinched her button nose between his thumb and index finger, and said, "Okay then, little sis."

He turned to give Demi the same loving squeeze, but she held up her hand and said, "If you come within an inch from me with those dirty fingers after a weekend at the bend, you'd better be ready to lose that finger."

He laughed with his head back. "I feel sorry for John. Poor guy."

Demi jutted her chin. "He's lucky to have me. I'm a catch."

Amara and Zeus shared a smile. Demi could sound so tough and entitled. Almost like an Old Lady of IVMC. But in truth, she was a harmless teddy bear.

Despite of their protests, he slung an arm over his sisters' shoulders and said, "I'm the lucky one. I got to have the two of you."

Amara elbowed him in his ribs. "You're such a wuss."

Demi giggled and Zeus laughed along. It relieved some of the weight on his chest.

"Love you, too." Amara said. After a beat she added, "I know we shouldn't have heard anything about what's been going on between you and Dad… But can you promise me something?"

His gut churned. "I can't promise you anything, sis."

He already knew what Amara was heading for. And he couldn't promise her a damn thing about their father's future.

Because what his sisters didn't know—but he did, was that

their father not only had turned into an unpredictable drug addict with anger management issues.

He'd caused the death of four people.

Annas had betrayed the club.

And one could never walk away from betraying the club.

Not unscathed, that is.

7

Z eus glanced over at the live feed of the security camera pointed at Ronan Mills. Ronan stood outside of the door at the end of the back hallway of the clubhouse, where they often met friends of the club who weren't allowed into their sacred room where they held church.

When Ronan called Devlin for a meeting, Zeus instantly knew he wouldn't sit out in the bar with him. He had a sick feeling to his stomach that this meeting wasn't about that sewer rat, Hank, stabbing Ronan a few weeks ago.

"Come in," Zeus said.

Ronan entered, his eyes scanning Zeus and Demon sitting at the oval table in the middle of the room. His gaze went over the motorcycle parts that hung on the back wall of the room, before he took in the two couches and a coffee table to the side.

When Ronan inspected the long rows of mug shots that covered the entire right wall, Zeus had enough and said, "Have a seat."

As his fellow MMA fighter in their underground fight club, Devlin knew Ronan best out of anyone in the club. Zeus understood why Ronan had reached out to Devlin first. But since Devlin wasn't in the know about their club leaders dealing drugs and causing the attack by the cartel, Zeus had chosen to keep Devlin out of this meeting.

Demon sat next to Zeus at the oval table and he jerked his chin at Ronan in greeting. Wolf stood next to the door, keeping an eye out on the security feed.

"Where's Dev?" Ronan asked.

"He's unavailable at the moment…" Wolf said behind Ronan.

Ronan hung around the club for so long, he almost felt like a club brother. But the fact that he wasn't, made whatever they would talk about extra precarious. Zeus wanted Ronan to feel out of his comfort zone. He needed to be able to read him because there was too much at stake here.

"I'm only talkin' with Dev present. Not sayin' I don't trust you. But for this matter, I want Dev around."

Shit. Ronan would drop another bomb on his doorstep tonight. Zeus just knew it. He was glad his dad left the club with Silas to go on a run nobody in the club knew dick about. Zeus nodded at Wolf, who went out into the hallway to get Devlin.

"I don't like people coming into the club making demands, Ronan. It's solely because I have a feeling about what you're about to tell me, that I'll grant you this one request."

"Appreciate it, Zeus."

All three of them kept quiet until Devlin meandered into the room and Wolf closed the door behind him, taking back his spot at the wall behind Ronan.

"Hey, man. You wanted to talk about something?" Devlin said, sitting down next to Demon. Ronan scrutinized Zeus a moment before he watched Demon bringing a hand through his half-long black hair.

"Okay. Out with it," Demon said.

Ronan took a deep breath before he said, "A little birdy told me it's snowing right on the club's doorstep."

Motherfucker. If even one of their underground fighters knew, then there was no way there weren't others who knew about their club leaders going rogue. Zeus swallowed down his emotions as he stared at the bringer of this shit news.

"Fuckin' hell," Devlin said, searching the room for anyone else being thrown for a loop, but Wolf and Demon kept any surprise from their stone-cold faces.

Demon cracked his knuckles in front of his face with his elbows resting on the tabletop. "Did your little birdy say anything else?"

Ronan wasn't in the least intimidated by Demon. His eyes narrowed as he said, "That the person who's spreading this snow all over town got it from your club. He's the one who stabbed me. But you probably already knew that."

Everyone in the underworld talked about Hank, some low-life small time drug dealer, stabbing Ronan. Hank was still somewhere in hiding, like some scared little bitch. That was indeed old news. But what they didn't know was that Hank dealt drugs coming from their own motherfucking clubhouse.

"We didn't. You'll need to give us more info, Ro," Zeus said.

"Nah. That's all I got," Ronan said, and he stood from the table.

Wolf pushed Ronan back into his seat with a firm hand on his shoulder. "Have a seat. Zeus said nothing about being done."

"Look. I'm not a member of the MC. I'm not even a hangaround. I respect your club and I'm willin' to go a long way with you, but if this fucker doesn't take his filthy hand from my shoulder within the next three seconds, I'm goin' to slam my fist into his windpipe."

Zeus' upper lip pulled at the fearlessness of Ronan Mills. He knew there was a reason he'd always liked the guy. Demon actually laughed next to him, somewhat breaking the tension in the room.

Wolf took his hand away and Ronan grumbled, "Good. I have something else to tell you. I'm quitting the fight club. I'm done with everything. I've got a woman now and I'm not willing to risk her safety. So this," he whirled his index finger around the room, "has to stay far away from me and mine."

"Who's the broad?" Wolf asked.

"Non of your business," Ronan spat over his shoulder.

"Is it my sister?" Devlin leaned in on his under arms resting on the tabletop, probably making sure they were still on the same page and Ronan wasn't messing around. Instead of answering, Ronan took in Demon who fought hard to keep his restraint.

Demon said in a carefully controlled tone of voice, "Catriona?"

Ronan laughed. He probably saw right through Demon even though he tried to hide his interest in Catriona.

"No. One of my half-sisters: Fianna," Devlin said.

Demon and Ronan stared at each other across the oval table. "Fair enough. I reckon you're out for months to recover from surgery, anyway," Demon said.

"That's not your call to make, Enforcer," Zeus said. It wasn't like Demon to speak out of turn. His feelings for Devlin's sister, Catriona, must be really messing with him.

"She means that much to you, eh?" Zeus asked Ronan. The club was about to lose one of their best fighters—if not the best. Zeus should have been bummed out since it wasn't good for business for their underground fight club bookies and live streams. But Zeus understood where Ronan was coming from. If anything, this past year had shown Zeus that life was too short to have any regrets.

"Yes. Fi is my life. I'm done," Ronan said.

"Okay. You've fought your last match for us. But that doesn't mean our dealings are over," Zeus said as he leaned in over the table, his palms flat on the table.

"Wait. Why?" Ronan said, and his brows furrowed.

"I'm not letting you leave this room until you tell us exactly what we want to know. Tell us what your brother found out about the guy that stabbed you."

Ronan's brother Donovan was a well-known and respected PI, and Zeus had heard from the club's computer tech, Fox, how Donovan could hack into almost every system. He figured Donovan would look into his brother's attacker.

Zeus scrutinized Ronan's facial reaction. Ronan tried to close himself off from Zeus, but he still noticed how Ronan struggled with making the decision to tell them everything his brother had found out.

Ronan took a moment too long to give them answers, so Demon said, "That fucking idiot has been in hiding ever since he cut you open like he wanted to sell you for parts. Hank's a real piece of work. Apparently, he called his cousin last night and told her he wants revenge for being chased out of Austin."

By sharing this information with Ronan, Demon probably tried to pave the way for Ronan to trust them enough to spill the beans. Demon was full on in enforcer mode now and said, "Who's been meeting up with Hank? You said it's snowing on our doorstep. Someone from our club is supplying Hank with blow."

Zeus already figured that their President and VP handled the drug supply. It had to be them. All they needed for a throw down was some hard evidence—something Silas and Annas couldn't dispute.

Ronan didn't respond fast enough, and Zeus slammed his fist on the table. "If you weren't a friend of the club, we would have had this conversation in our fuckin' basement with a drain in the middle of the fuckin' floor. Now fuckin' tell us who's been doin' us dirty!"

"Silas."

Demon gave Zeus a nod. This was it. If Donovan had found something on Hank and Silas, they could use it to their benefit. They could bring this before the club members and get Annas and Silas out in bad standing.

Devlin's chair scraped over the floor as he got up from his seat. "What?"

Yeah. That was exactly how Zeus figured the rest of their club would react to this news.

"Sit down." Zeus said to Devlin, and added, "And whatever the fuck has been said stays in this room."

Even though he trusted Devlin with his life, he wasn't an officer of the club. Zeus needed to make sure Devlin knew what they expected of him.

Devlin plunked down in his seat. "He's our VP, Z. What the fuck, man?"

"Not with an outsider present, Dev," Demon said in a calm tone of voice.

Ronan held up both hands. "I'll take that as my cue to leave you guys to it."

"I'll walk you out," Zeus said. He held still in the hallway for a moment and said in a hushed voice to Ronan, "Thank you for comin' to us. I'll not forget how you gave us a heads-up about somethin' others might have walked away from. If you ever need us, give us a call, okay?"

It was a rare thing for Zeus to hand out markers. But in this case, it felt like the only right thing to do. Snitching about the VP's involvement to his club brothers could have had a deadly ending for Ronan. Zeus appreciated Ronan had stuck out his neck for him.

"Come, let's get us some beers," Zeus said as he walked into the bar.

Turtle sat on a barstool, flagging over Ronan. "Ro! I've been meaning to talk with you 'bout somethin'."

Zeus arched a brow at Ronan, not knowing what this old hoot was up to now. Turtle hooked his leathered arm around Zion's neck. "It's about my man Zion here."

Everyone knew Zion was bisexual. Zeus smiled at Ronan's discomfort, as it seemed for a second like Turtle tried to set Ronan up with Zion.

"Talked to your girls that day we visited you in the hospital…" Turtle said.

"Ah, you've talked to Gwenn, eh?" Ronan chuckled.

"Zion's been daydreaming about her dirty mouth ever since."

"Shut up, Turtle." Zion rolled his eyes and said, "It's the other way around. Ever since that pretty thing talked about his eight-foot schlong, Turtle's done nothing but talkin' 'bout her."

A few brothers listening in on them busted out laughing.

"Who's Gwenn?" Zeus asked Ronan.

"My partner at Mills PI and Security. She's also my woman's sister and one of my best friends. So you guys better watch your mouths, okay?"

It was the second time he heard about this Gwenn chick. Back at the bend, Devlin had told him that Gwenn Ryan, his half-sister, had served in Afghanistan.

Turtle waved a hand in the air and said, "Brass Balls doesn't need you to defend her honor, Ro. She's man enough to handle us lot."

Ronan laughed. "Brass Balls? You gave her a road name already, huh?"

That these guys already gave Gwenn a road name told Zeus that she somehow had earned their respect. That was no small feat.

After a few drinks, Zeus left his brothers in the bar and went up to his room on the second floor. He wouldn't do anything with this information about Silas and Hank. Not tonight.

He undressed in his room and turned off the lights. He rolled onto his side and tried to get some sleep. Tomorrow, he would have a talk with Wolf and Demon. Try to work on a plan to take over the club.

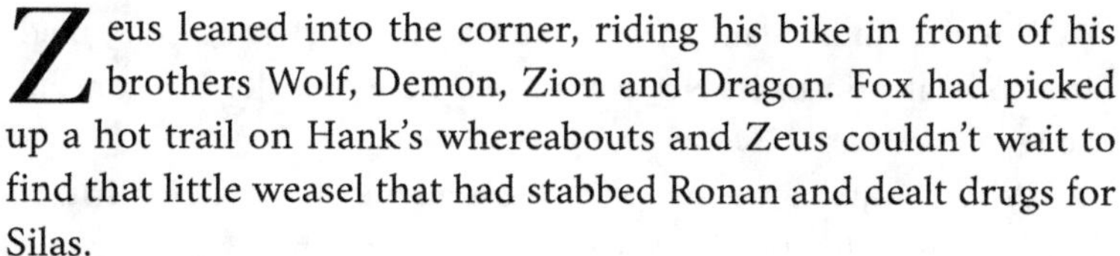

8

Zeus leaned into the corner, riding his bike in front of his brothers Wolf, Demon, Zion and Dragon. Fox had picked up a hot trail on Hank's whereabouts and Zeus couldn't wait to find that little weasel that had stabbed Ronan and dealt drugs for Silas.

With Silas and Annas both still out on a run, now would be a perfect time to bring in Hank for a moment of truth in the club's basement.

The nimble and powerful machine between Zeus' legs made the adrenaline rush through his veins. He revved his engine when he recognized Ronan's truck ahead. That damn Irish bastard drove straight ahead over the winding, deserted dusty road to the fenced-up warehouse Zeus was heading for.

The moment Ronan had parked his truck, a dark-haired whirlwind hopped out. The shiny chestnut hair of the woman swept over her shoulder as she took a few steps away from the truck.

He overheard Ronan say something to this woman about searching for Hank and not being there for a pissing match with the MC. He figured that this must be the infamous Gwenn Ryan, Ronan's private investigations partner.

Before he could take a good look at her, she surprised him

when she said to Ronan, "Oh, hush. We all know women can't win in a pissing match. It's only because we don't have a hose to put our piss further."

Zeus heard a few snickers behind him from his brothers that also had just parked their bikes. His eyes zeroed in on her scuffed and discolored combat boots and went up to her tight black jeans. Her customized belt below her flat stomach caught his eye.

His best friend must have noticed the same thing as Demon said, "You got a permit for that gun at your back?"

The most sparkling azure eyes Zeus had ever seen twinkled before him with mischief. "Who wants to know?" she asked, raising a brow.

When Demon leaned in to take a step forward, Zeus made sure to beat him to it. No way in hell he would let Demon take the lead. Not with Gwenn.

"What's your name, sweets?" he asked her to test her spirit. He didn't know why, but he got instantly hard when she narrowed her eyes at him. He liked playing with her, teasing her for more fire to come out blazing. He smiled and said, "Cat got your tongue…?"

To Zeus' surprise, she took a full step forward so she would be within arms' reach of him. Not what he expected from a five-foot nine woman, standing eye to eye with a six-foot seven Sergeant-at-Arms and four other members of a motorcycle club at his back.

He heard rustling behind his back, like someone grabbed for their weapon. Gwenn clicked her tongue and said, "Why are men so disappointing?"

Ronan did the introductions and Dragon and Zion argued about a road name for Gwenn. Zeus felt annoyed but he couldn't pin point the reason why. Was it because he felt like he had missed out on meeting her earlier? Or was it because seeing Gwenn squaring off did something to him. Something he hadn't felt before.

From the moment she'd hopped out of that truck, he wanted to grab her jaw in his hand and take her mouth. He wanted to wrap her ponytail around his fist, and direct their kiss so that he could seize her. Her spirit and fearless attitude stirred something animalistic inside of him.

"Gwenn and I are going to check out the warehouse for a second," Ronan said.

"Why?" Demon crossed his arms in front of his leather cut.

"We've got a lead on some boring PI job. That okay… Stud?"

Zeus fought the urge to growl at Gwenn for calling his best friend Stud. He needed to get his head back in the game. They were out here on a job. They needed to find the asshole who dealt drugs for Silas. He needed to bring Silas down and make his father stand down and hand over the gavel.

He hadn't got the time for this sexy little minx that sparked something inside of him that he thought was long gone.

"You do know that this is a knowing hang out spot for the Strong Riders MC? I don't believe they would want to have two civilians sniffin' around," Zeus said.

The bastards of the Strong Riders MC formed a piece of shit club, worming their way into Iron Vikings territory in the past six months. They were the worst one-percenters. No respect for club rules and no respect for women as they also traded in skin.

Zeus closed the distance between him and Gwenn. As they stood toe-to-toe, he leaned in and whispered, "If I say you're in, then you're in. But I'll be watching every sway of your delectable ass."

Gwenn whirled on the balls of her feet and strutted over to the chain-link fence that had been opened by Zion. He followed her inside the crestfallen warehouse. She gave him a scary grin, and he immediately forgave himself for acting like a love-sick puppy.

She tried to scare him away by acting all tough and rough around the edges. But what she didn't realize was that her attitude, mixed with her heart stopping beauty and sexiness, already had drawn him in.

The dim interior of the warehouse made him aware of his mission today. He snapped out of it when Gwenn suddenly dropped on one knee and grabbed her gun from her holster at her lower back. "Get down!" she shouted.

Zeus did as she said and pulled out his gun. He signaled to a crouching Demon next to the left sidewall to hold still for a moment.

Gwenn held out her hand, pointing her fingers like a gun. She turned her hand upside down and pointed to the left, a few feet away from Demon. Zeus hadn't served, but he knew that her gesture meant she had someone in sight. This person must have been standing right in the line of Demon's fire and vice versa.

"Shit…" he whispered.

Gwenn crouched to the right side of the warehouse before he could stop her.

"Fuckin' G.I. Jane," Wolf murmured next to him.

Although this brick wall warehouse seemed to be abandoned, the few storage racks to the sides were ideal spots for someone to play hide and seek.

The click of a safety being pulled echoed against the bare, high walls of the warehouse. He heard several feet away at his far left side Gwenn's voice as she said, "Drop your gun, handsome."

He made his way over to her voice and found Demon standing with his mouth slack like he'd just seen a ghost. Gwenn pointed her gun at Hank, who seemed to have sneaked up on Demon.

"Can you believe this motherfucker? What in the hell were you even trying to do against all of us if you'd killed him?" Zeus roared. He couldn't believe how close they were in losing not only another member, but also his best friend.

Gwenn lowered her gun and she slid Hank's weapon to the side with her foot.

"Nice work, G.I. Jane," Wolf said as he picked up Hank's gun.

Zeus growled, "Shut the fuck up." He had enough of his brothers making up road names for Gwenn. If anyone, he would be the one to give her a road name. Damn it.

He got so worked up that he sucker punched Hank, as he clearly couldn't hit Wolf over something this irrational.

As Hank fell to the ground, he turned to Gwenn and said, "You did good, baby girl."

Something happened that blew his socks off. The sweetest pink colored blush crept over Gwenn's apple cheeks. Seeing this softer side of her made his dick weep in his jeans. He wanted to own that softer side. Be the only one to get glimpses of that enigma.

"I thought you were watching every sway of my delectable ass? How come you sound so surprised I showed up on this side?" she said and smiled mischievously.

"Enough! Your flirting is giving me a headache," Demon rumbled.

"It's giving me a hard on," Zion said and grabbed his crotch. "Fuck. Did you see her stalk him with that gun in hand? I wanted to—"

Without giving it a second thought, Zeus took Zion by his throat and lifted his six-foot three body from the ground.

"One. More. Word."

Zion turned red in the face before he held up both hands in defeat.

Demon understood that whatever was going on with Zeus, was important enough to go at Zion's throat, as he added, "Show some fuckin' respect."

Wolf tried to defuse the situation and said, "Okay. Devlin is two minutes out with the van."

Demon knocked Hank unconscious, and Zeus said, "Can you take him outside? I want to talk to Gwenn for a moment."

Ronan tried to square off to Zeus, but Gwenn said, "It's okay, Ro. I'll be right out."

Ronan must have figured he could scare away Zeus from Gwenn as he said, "Just so you know; she's not only my woman's sister. She's also Devlin's sister."

"You've got to be fuckin' kiddin' me," Zeus said. He couldn't believe Ronan would have the nerve to bring up that club rule. Zeus knew like no other he needed to stay away from a brother's sister. But fuckin' hell. This felt different.

As they were the only two left in the enormous warehouse, the silence became deafening. He stared into her sky-blue eyes, memorizing the shape and color.

"Okay. You've got me alone and all you want to do is stare into my eyes? What's next? You want to hold hands and sing a song?"

He snorted at her obvious attempt to rile him up so he would leave her the fuck alone. As one fucked-up soul he recognized one standing in front of him. He knew all the reasons why he should stay away from her.

He'd buried his Old Lady just six months ago. His lifestyle had always been dangerous, but if he would take over the gavel from his father, shit would hit the fan. There was no way there wouldn't be any blowback. He wouldn't take any risk with Gwenn. He wasn't the same egotistical asshole he used to be.

"Nah. Just wanted to have one last look at you, baby girl."

She redid her ponytail, her elbows pointing toward the ceiling and her breasts almost popping out of her tight fitted tank top. Shit. She enticed him even without trying.

"One last look?"

"Yeah. You're not my type, sweets. But you're a looker. I have to give you that." He hoped that she would be smart enough to leave things well enough alone.

"Arrogant asshole." She said before she stomped out of the warehouse.

He knew he'd done the right thing. There was a war coming. And a war meant casualties. If his enemies knew how much she affected him after only seeing her once, her life would be in danger. And the target on her back would be gigantic if he did what he wanted to do from the second she'd squared off at him outside the warehouse: make her his.

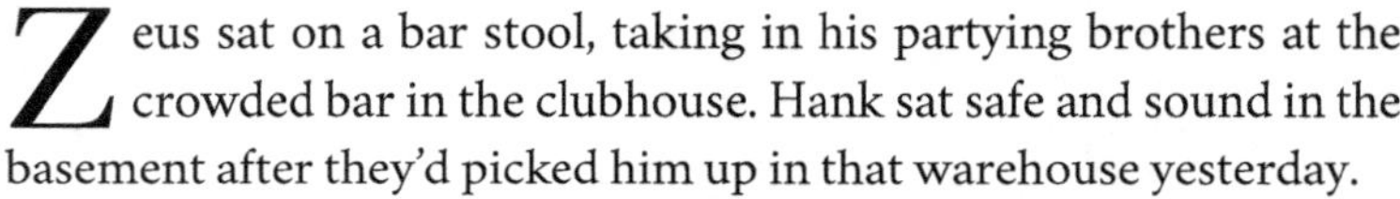

9

Zeus sat on a bar stool, taking in his partying brothers at the crowded bar in the clubhouse. Hank sat safe and sound in the basement after they'd picked him up in that warehouse yesterday.

Well, he sat in the basement. Hank wasn't exactly safe in this lions' den. And after Demon had a heart-to-heart with him, Hank wasn't exactly sound either. He did have a few interesting things to say about Silas, though.

Apparently, they met every Wednesday near that alley where Hank stabbed Ronan. Zeus couldn't believe Silas' audacity to use his murdered daughter as an excuse to go to her grave every Wednesday, while in truth he actually met Hank so he could sell cartel drugs on the streets.

Hank's words and Donovan Mills' footage of Silas and Hank meetings were all that Zeus needed to get the rest of the club involved. It was up to Zeus to put a stop to his father's reign. Nobody else was going to do it. His friends said it was Zeus' place since he would be the next President.

Zeus took a pull from his beer. He couldn't believe this shit. He needed to calm down. He had no idea when his father would come back from his run.

But when his father would come back, he would do something unheard of in their club: Zeus would ask his brothers to turn their backs on his father and to set the President and VP out of the club in bad standing.

Zeus' phone buzzed in his pocket and he picked up without screening the call. "Zeus."

He recognized Ronan's voice immediately and strained his ears to follow Ronan over the loud rock music of the clubhouse bar.

"I need your help. Some guys from another MC just snatched Fianna and Gwenn."

Without thinking, Zeus threw his barstool over the bar, shattering bottles lined up on a couple of shelves. Gisele and Allison screamed and the music instantly stopped.

"Damn it, Zeus. What the hell is wrong with you?" Turtle shouted next to him.

Zeus didn't care for his brothers eyeing him up and down, trying to figure out why he would flip his shit like this. He concentrated on his phone call.

"Who?" Zeus said in a demanding voice. He waved at Devlin to follow him. Wolf and Demon flanked his sides as they walked out of the clubhouse and into the dark courtyard between the clubhouse and Vikings Auto Salvage. He got on his bike, not starting the engine just yet. He put his phone on speaker so Devlin, Demon and Wolf could listen in.

Dragon followed Angel, Fox, Crusher and Zion outside, his eyes zeroing in on Zeus sitting on his motorcycle, ready to roar out of there.

"My cousin was there. She didn't know what to look for. They seemed bikers, and they had some kind of emblem with the word 'Strong' in it," Ronan said on speaker.

Demon mouthed, "Gwenn?" Zeus nodded.

"That's no coincidence, Ro. Think about it. We've picked up Hank at an abandoned warehouse that's been used as Strong

Riders MC's graveyard. You remember those fields behind that warehouse?"

As he said it, Zeus felt the chills running up his spine. That damn eerie place was a perfect spot to hide two women they'd taken. Gwenn and her sister, Fianna, were in the hands of the same sick fuckers who sell women to the highest bidders like it was no skin off their back.

Zeus' ears drummed and bile clawed its way up his throat. Not that long ago, Silas had said that the Strong Riders MC were a joke—that they shouldn't take them seriously. He wondered if Silas had ulterior motives to let Strong Riders MC play around in their own backyard. He also wondered if his father had anything to do with kidnapping Fianna and Gwenn.

"They've got Fi and Gwenn, Z. We need to go. This just happened like ten minutes ago."

Ronan hung up the phone and Zeus shot out of the parking lot, leading the way for his brothers. The wind against his face sobered Zeus. He didn't know what his next step would be if they didn't find Gwenn at this warehouse. The time to confront his father would come sooner than later. It was time to step up as the President of Iron Vikings MC.

He arrived at the warehouse and killed his engine. Dragon, Demon and Zeus crept closer to the entrance of the warehouse. He sent Angel, Wolf, Crusher, Zion and Fox to the back of the site where they slipped through a hole in the fence.

Before he could stop him, Devlin sneaked inside from the front. He wasn't willing to waste any time.

From the other side of the tall grass, Ronan joined Zeus and his group. Ronan watched Devlin slipping inside the warehouse and without even a word or a heads-up, Ronan followed Devlin inside.

Zeus had no control whatsoever over this entire operation. His head was all over the place as he kept envisioning all the horrible things Gwenn and her sister could be going through.

Dragon slapped Zeus back, startling him. It brought him out of his head and into the present. He joined his brothers inside the warehouse and held still in shock at the sight before him.

A guy lay motionless on his back, in front of the right back tire of a black van. A piece of wood stuck out of the guy's neck. If he had to guess, the man had bled to death—going by the amount of blood that had pooled around him on the concrete floor.

"The van is empty, Z. No sign of the girls," Demon said.

"My guess is that your girl got to this fucker," Dragon said as he toed the dead man's leg with his combat boot.

Zeus didn't correct Dragon. He was about to hunt and kill every single Strong Rider if he wouldn't find Gwenn in the next few minutes.

The fearful scream coming from the waist-length tall grass next to the warehouse would be forever ingrained in his head. It sounded like a woman's last cry for help. Like she knew her last seconds in this life had been ticking away.

Devlin ran through the grass, Ronan and Zeus hot on his trail.

They heard rustling in the grass to their right. Devlin ran a few yards before he dove upon some guy, holding a frightened redhead down in the grass and balling his fist like he wanted to knock her lights out.

Ronan picked up this woman, soothing her. Devlin knocked the Strong Rider biker around and said, "Shut the fuck up, you piece of shit!"

Zeus' eyes frantically searched the grass. There was no sign of Gwenn. By the looks of the scratches and bewildered eyes of Ronan's girlfriend, Fianna, Zeus' stomach dropped. What if they were too late?

"Where is she?" Zeus roared. He startled Fianna, but she waved into the opposite direction as where he'd come from. He ran through the grass, and almost tripped over Gwenn's motionless body.

A cold sweat broke out as he kneeled next to her. "Gwenn… Gwenn…."

She groaned and opened her eyes. She blinked a few times like she couldn't believe she actually was alive.

When she tried to talk, he said, "Shh. It's okay. Fianna's safe. You are safe. I've got you, baby girl."

Gwenn's eyes rolled back in her head as he picked her up from the cold ground. He walked straight ahead, to Squirrel's van. He was thankful that at least one of his brothers still had his wits about him to call in the prospect.

"Someone call Doc. Tell him to meet me at my room in the clubhouse. No one breathes a word about what happened here tonight. Not a fuckin' word, you got me?" Zeus said to no one in particular, knowing he had his brothers' undivided attention, anyway.

He slipped into the back of the van with Gwenn in his arms. He pushed some chestnut strands of hair from her face as he examined the cuts and bruises. Even with one eye completely swollen shut, blood smeared all over her face, caking into her hairline and her lips busted open: she was still the most beautiful woman he'd ever seen because of that fire inside of her that still blinded him.

That same spark, that fighter's spirit was probably what had saved her life tonight. He was in awe of this woman. He hadn't spoken more than a few sentences to her when they met earlier. Most of it had been about him showing off. Making sure she knew he was the top dog in his world.

As he glanced down at Gwenn, he had no idea what was in store for them. All he knew was how much she affected him. How he wouldn't trust anyone else but him to take care of her. She would stay with him in his room and get back on her feet.

Getting Gwenn back safely in his arms wasn't their happily ever after. He knew what was waiting for them at his clubhouse.

This wasn't over.

Not by a long shot.

* * *

THANK you for reading this **PREQUEL**! If you enjoyed this novella, please consider leaving a review. It's reviews from fans like you that help spread the word about my books.

CLICK HERE to leave a rating or a review.

DO you want to know what happens next in Zeus' road to presidency and how Gwenn will react waking up in Zeus' bed in the clubhouse? Continue with book 1 in the series: **Zeus**

AND DID Demon spark your interest? Pre-order his steamy age-gap romance here: **Demon**

HAVE YOU READ THE SEXY, heartfelt and funny Lucky Irish series? MMA fighter Ronan is book 6 in the series: **Ronan**

AND IVMC MEMBER Devlin is book 7 in the Lucky Irish series: **Devlin**

HAVE you heard of the Winter Peaks series about the Mills cousins in Winter Peaks, Colorado? **Winter Peaks series**

ALSO BY ANNA CASTOR

Iron Vikings MC:

Prequel - Iron Vikings MC 0.5

Zeus - Iron Vikings MC 1

Demon - Iron Vikings MC 2

Lucky Irish series:

Book 1 - Duncan (Kayla & Duncan)

Book 2 - Donovan (Kate & Donovan)

Book 3 - Brennan (Errin & Brennan)

Book 4 - Declan (Bree & Declan)

Book 5 - Keenan (Ryleigh & Keenan)

Book 6 - Ronan (Fianna & Ronan)

Book 7 - Devlin (Devlin & Teagan)

Winter Peaks series:

Book 1 - Adam (Caitlin & Adam)

Book 2 - Damian (Chloe & Damian)

Book 3 - Matteo (Lily & Matteo)

Book 4 - Owen (Tara & Owen)

AUDIOBOOKS:

Audiobook Duncan (Lucky Irish Book 1)

ACKNOWLEDGMENTS

A huge thank you to all of the amazing readers and fans out there who took a chance on reading one of my books! I'm so excited to share my books with you!

Thank you to all the reviewers, ARC readers and bloggers who've helped me to get the word out! I'm so grateful for all your support!

Dear Lauren, we did it again! Thank you for joining me on this ride :) I'm so grateful to have your help and guidance to explore this whole new world of IVMC. Your ideas and tips are awesome and have helped me through nervous breakdowns and writer's block on more than one occasion. You keep me sane and help making my stories shine! Thank you!

Thank you Roxana for proofreading this Prequel and helping me out! It's been great working with you :)

To my family, my husband and three daughters, you give me so much inspiration on writing about love and strong-willed heroines in particular. Every day, you make me feel so loved, and I can only hope that I'm making you proud.

ANNA CASTOR

Anna Castor is the author of the Lucky Irish series, Winter Peaks series and Iron Vikings MC series. She loves to write heartfelt & sexy romance series with close-knit families, strong heroines & alpha hotness

She has a soft spot for sexy small town romances, sports romances and motorcycle romances.

Favorite things to write are the banter between siblings but also the real talk that comes with family. There's no hiding from a nosy Pops

Anna lives in a small town near Amsterdam, The Netherlands, with her husband and their three daughters. When she's not writing and has some time left between bringing her kids to school and picking them up from play dates or volleyball practice, she's glued to her e-reader.

A weird fact about Anna: every time she takes a piece of chewing gum; the mint makes her sneeze.

Anna loves to hear from her readers <3.

Follow her online to get updates on new releases, ARC opportunities, freebies and more!

Connect with her online:

Website: www.annacastor.com